Here's a story to share!

Sharing a story with your child is great fun and it's an ideal way to start your child reading.

The left-hand pages are 'your' story pages. The right-hand pages are specially written for your child with simple vocabulary and helpful repetition.

• Cuddle up close and look through the book together. What's happening in the pictures?

• Read the whole story to your child, both your story pages and your child's. Tell your child what it says on his* story pages and point to the words as you say them.

• Now it's time to read the story again and see if your child would like to join in and read his story pages along with you. Don't worry about perfect reading – what matters at this stage is having fun.

• It's best to stop when your child wants to. You can pick up the book at any time and enjoy sharing the story all over again.

Here the child is referred to as 'he'. All Ladybird books are equally suitable for both boys and girls.

Edited by Lorraine Horsley and Caroline Rashleigh
Designed by Alison Guthrie, Lara Stapleton and Graeme Hole
A catalogue record for this book is available from the British Library

Published by Ladybird Books Ltd
27 Wrights Lane London W8 5TZ
A Penguin Company

2 4 6 8 10 9 7 5 3 1

TEXT © MARTIN WADDELL MCMXCI
ILLUSTRATIONS © JANE MASSEY MMI
First published by Viking MCMXCI
Published in Picture Puffins MCMXCII
This edition published by Ladybird Books Ltd MMI
LADYBIRD and the device of a Ladybird are trademarks of Ladybird Books Ltd

Man Mountain

by Martin Waddell
illustrated by Jane Massey

Oscar was the last of the Giants.
He was very lonely.
He lay down and went to sleep.
There were hurricanes and storms and
floods and twisters and volcanoes, but
Oscar just slept on. For ever, almost.

A big mouth.

17

"I'll just jump off, shall I?" said Rose, and she hopped off into Beard Forest, where she landed in a tree, and had to climb down.

She found Matthew. They clung to each other as the forest rocked and shook. Then the shaking stopped.

"Now we can get away!" Rose said.

But Oscar heard her.

SPLOSH!

A big splash.

Oscar's voice was so loud that people in Ankle village heard it.

They came up Man Mountain to find Matthew and Rose.

"What's that noise, Rose?" they said.

"It's Oscar's Giant Stories. Stay and hear them."

And all the children did.

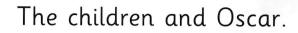

The children and Oscar.

The children from Ankle village came again and again, so Oscar wasn't lonely any more.

And neither was Rose.

Oscar, Rose, Matthew
and the children.

Turn off the TV, close the door, too.
Here's a story to share for just me and you...

Inky-pinky blot

Who is the inky-pinky blot in the dark, dark pond? He asks everyone who goes by, but no one ever seems to know...

Caterpillars can't fly!

A baby caterpillar dreams of flying high in the sky but all her friends just laugh. What is she to do?

By the light of the Moon

Charlie the zoo keeper has gone home and the zoo is quiet. Now it's time for the animals to dance by the light of the moon...

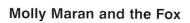

Molly Maran and the Fox

It's cold outside and Molly the kind-hearted hen says all the animals can stay in her warm barn. But how will she keep out the wily fox?